Not I, Not I

Modern Curriculum Press
BEGINNING
TO
READ
Series

Not I, Not I

Margaret Hillert

Illustrated by Diana Magnuson

MODERN CURRICULUM PRESS

Cleveland • Toronto

Not I, Not I

Published by Modern Curriculum Press, Inc.
13900 Prospect Road, Cleveland, Ohio 44136

Library of Congress Cataloging in Publication Data

Hillert, Margaret.
  Not I, not I.

Summary: The little red hen finds none of her lazy friends willing to help her plant, harvest or
grind wheat into flour, but all are eager to eat the bread she makes from it.

(1. Folklore)   I. Magnuson, Diana.   II. Title.   III. Title: Little red hen.

PZ8.1.H539No   398.2′452′861   (E)   79-23847

ISBN 0-8136-5563-3 Paperback
ISBN 0-8136-5063-1 Hardbound

Library of Congress Catalog Card Number: 79-23847

1 2 3 4 5 6 7 8 9 10   89 88 87 86

Here is a mother.
The mother is little.
The mother is red.

Look here.
Here is a little baby.
The baby is yellow.
It can run and play.

See the yellow baby run.
See it run to Mother.
It said, "Mother, Mother.
I want something."

Mother said, "Come and look.
Help me find something.
Away we go."

Look, look.

Here is something.

Something little.

I can work.

I can make it big.

9

Oh, oh.
Look here.
One, two, three.
Can you help me?

11

Not I.
Not I.
Not I.
We can not help.

12

I can.

I can work.

See it go down here.

14

Look, look.
See where it is.
It is up.
It is big, big, big.

Can you help?
Can you three help me?
Come and work.

16

Not I.
Not I.
Not I.
We can not help.

19

It is funny.
You can not work.
You can not help.
I can work.

Here I go.
Away, away.
Can you come?
Can you help?

Not I.
Not I.
Not I.
We can not help.

See, see.

It is in here.

I can make something.

I can work.

See me work.

I can make something.

Look here, baby.
It can go in here.
It is for you.

Here it is.
Come and look.
Oh, oh.
Can you help me?

I can.
I can.
I can.
We can help.

Oh, oh.
We see it.
We want it.

29

30

Not you.
Not you.
Not you.
Go away.
It is for my little baby and me.

Margaret Hillert, author and poet, has written many books for young readers. She is a former first-grade teacher and lives in Birmingham, Michigan.

Not I, Not I uses the 44 words listed below.

a	help	oh	up
and	here	one	
away			want
	I	play	we
baby	in		where
big	is	red	work
	it	run	
can			yellow
come	little	said	you
	look	see	
down		something	
	make		
find	me	the	
for	mother	three	
funny	my	to	
		two	
go	not		